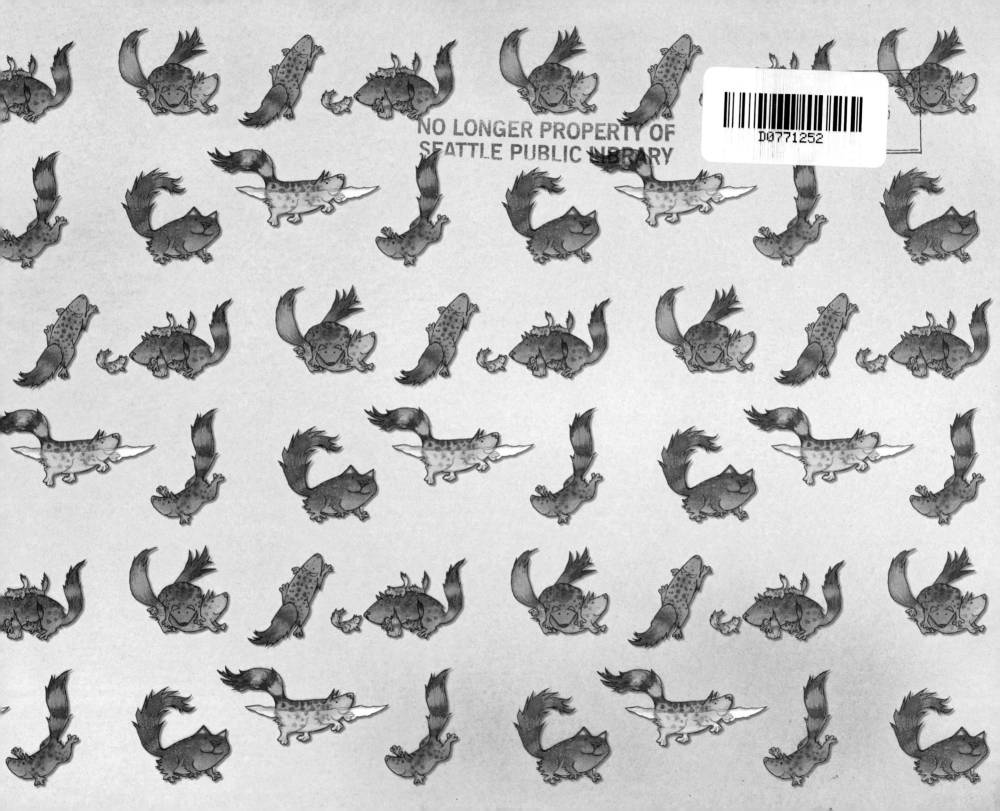

For my beloved grandma, Martha Schultz,
and my wandering angel, Kira Noelle,
who both make the sky more beautiful to gaze upon.
Special thanks to Terri Cohlene for her tremendous work on this story.
—HCS

To those who cherish, protect and celebrate all the plants and animals of earth.
—MGB

TOO MANY MURKLES

Story by Heidi Charissa Schmidt

Illustrations by Mary Gregg Byrne

ILLUMINATION
Arts
PUBLISHING COMPANY, INC.
Bellevue, Washington

It was the dreaded Day of the Murkles. Each year on this day, the people of Summerville gathered at the river to keep the horrible Murkles from entering their village.

Juliana stood with the townspeople as they formed their human wall. "Why do the Murkles keep coming back?" she asked.

The man beside her held a handkerchief to his face. "I don't know," he said. "I simply can't imagine what those stinky things want here."

As the Murkles waddled out of the river, a fine mist sprayed from the holes in their backs. Juliana pinched her nose. "That smells awful!"

The mayor's voice rang out. "Work together everybody. There are more than ever this year, but don't give up!"

Juliana stood firm until she felt a baby Murkle pawing at her leg. Kneeling down, she looked into its eyes. "Poor misunderstood little Murkle," Juliana whispered. "You just want a chance to make your journey, don't you?" Then she moved aside and let it wriggle past.

No one noticed, so Juliana followed the Murkle down Main Street. Blasting stinky mist, it wiggled along as if it knew where it was going.

Soon, they came to a pond where, with a soft hiss, the Murkle jumped into the cool water. Juliana watched as it splashed and played. Then it climbed onto a rock to sun itself, and something wonderful happened…

Juliana was so amazed she ran to find the mayor, who was holding off several of the largest creatures. "It's hopeless," he moaned. "This year, there are just too many Murkles."
Juliana tugged his sleeve. "Sir, I think I can solve the Murkle problem."

"You?" the mayor asked. "What could you possibly suggest?"
"Let them through," Juliana said. "Let them make the journey they want to make."
The mayor stared down at her. "What a crazy idea. Why should I listen to you?"
"Please trust me," she said. "Something wonderful will happen—you'll see."

"I give up," the mayor sighed. "There are so many Murkles, I suppose we might as well try your idea." Then he called out, "Let the Murkles pass!"

As the human wall parted, droves of Murkles waddled past the townfolk, down Main Street and into the pond, where they frolicked and swam. When the Murkles climbed out to sun themselves, mist again sprayed from their backs.

But this time something was different. The townspeople could hardly believe their noses—why, the air smelled of heavenly orange blossoms.

Everyone danced and cheered. "Hooray!" the mayor shouted. "From now on, there will never be too many Murkles!"

With the Murkle problem solved, the people of Summerville were much happier than before. Soon it was time to prepare for the county's Annual Garden Contest. "How wondrous!" the gardeners proclaimed. "The Murkle mist has made our grass greener, our sunflowers sunnier, and our roses rosier. We're sure to beat Foxdale this year!"

But that very afternoon, the mayor noticed a small red weed in the center of his perfect lawn. *Not a problem,* he thought. *I'll just snip it.*

By morning, however, there were dozens where the first had been. So he asked the president of the Summerville Gardeners' Club to look up the pest in a book. "Firestars," she read. "Rare, scarlet weeds. Nearly impossible to get rid of."

Soon the pesky things were growing everywhere. The townspeople tried everything they could think of. They tried potions. They tried poisons. They tried weed-stomping machines. But the determined Firestars kept right on polka-dotting the lawns of Summerville.

One morning, Juliana was staring at the Firestars. *Everyone is trying to solve this problem standing up,* she thought. *I shall try to solve it lying down.*

So she lay down on her own spotty lawn. "Poor, misunderstood little flowers," she said. You just want a chance to grow and spread out under the sun, don't you?"

At that, the Firestars stood a little taller.

Juliana ran to find the mayor again. "I know how to solve the Firestar problem," she declared.

The mayor raised one bushy eyebrow. "How?" he asked.

"You must let them be," she said. "For one whole week, do not stomp them, do not poison them—do not harm them at all."

The mayor thought for a moment. "We have tried everything else," he said, "so we may as well try this."

But after a few days, there were more Firestars than ever. "Fiddlesticks!" the people shouted. "The Firestars are taking over our town!" And it was true.

That evening, the mayor found Juliana. "Tomorrow is the day of the garden contest, and our lawns are completely covered by Firestars. Your idea didn't work. It didn't work at all!" Then he turned and walked away.

Juliana sighed. "Just wait and see," she whispered.

The next day when the judge arrived, all the townspeople were hiding. But then, something wonderful happened. "Oh, my," the judge exclaimed, "your lawns are gorgeous, like scarlet carpets!" And all the surprised townspeople stood a little straighter, just like the Firestars.

Summerville won the blue ribbon, and the next day Juliana was chosen Grand Marshal of the first ever Firestar Parade.

With Murkle mist in the air and Firestar lawns underfoot, the people of Summerville were even happier than before. But one day the mayor was watering his scarlet lawn when he noticed a dingy gray bird hovering about. The bird tilted its head and bellowed, SQUAWK–twi-LEEE–twi-LAWK.

"What an awful noise!" shouted the mayor. "Get out of here!" But the bird just kept screeching, SQUAWK–twi-LEEE–twi-LAWK. Then it dove at the lawn.

"Ack! My Firestars!" cried the mayor. "You will not ruin my peace AND my lawn!"

It was no use. Suddenly the strange birds were everywhere. The townspeople tried to chase them away, but the skies were full of the horrible creatures. What a din there was, and such a flapping of arms and wings.

Soon a crowd gathered around Town Hall, and someone called out, "What if they destroy our lawns?"

So the mayor called the president of the Birdwatchers' Society, who flipped through his guide book and stopped on page 472. "Ahhh," he said, "Tanzas. Very rare—attracted to bright colors."

A man with a face as red as his lawn shouted, "Tanzas, blanzas—I just want them gone!"

Again, people had lots of ideas. They tried sprays. They tried sprinklers. They tried scarecrows. But the Tanzas kept on squawking and swooping at the Firestars.

Finally the mayor caught one lone Tanza. Locked in a cage, it huddled, its beak tucked under one drab wing.

When Juliana saw the Tanza she knelt down. "Poor misunderstood little bird. You just want a chance to sing your song, don't you?"

The Tanza garbled a meek twi–lawk.

"You like bright colors, don't you?" Juliana pushed a Firestar through the bars. "Maybe this will cheer you."

Peering at her, the Tanza cautiously took the flower in its beak. Then something wonderful happened.

It was so amazing, Juliana ran to the mayor with her news. "I can solve the Tanza problem!"

This time the mayor smiled. "I'm not surprised. Tell me."

"You must let the Tanzas be," she said. "Do not chase them. Do not spray them. Do not yell at them. And please, set that poor bird free!"

The mayor shrugged. "You have been right before, Juliana. We will do as you suggest."

When the townspeople stopped all the shooing and shouting and waving, the Tanzas began to swoop. Each bird plucked a single Firestar then found a place to perch, tucking the flower under its wing. "Great," someone grumbled. "Now they've settled in."

"Shhhhhh…" Juliana said.

And when the people stopped fretting, something wonderful did happen…

The Tanzas tilted their heads and began to hum. The notes were softer than the whir of butterfly wings, like the whisper of rainbows.

Juliana's eyes prickled with tears as the Tanzas' quiet song spread over Summerville. Their feathers—once a dull gray—began to shimmer green and violet. The mayor hugged Juliana. "How did you know what to do?" he asked.

"I just got down on the ground," she said. "You see things a lot differently when you're eye-to-eye with a Tanza."

That night, the villagers were happier than ever before as they sat on their scarlet lawns listening to the sweet sounds and basking in the orange blossom mist. As for Juliana, the mayor asked her to be his assistant. She accepted, of course.

To this day, the people of Summerville still gather hand-in-hand at the edge of town, now to welcome the Murkles, and to celebrate the Firestars and Tanzas. But most of all, they celebrate Juliana, who taught them that the best way to solve a problem is to just get down and look it right in the eye.

ILLUMINATION Arts

PUBLISHING COMPANY, INC.

P.O. Box 1865 ◆ ellevue, WA 98009

Tel: 425-644-7185 ◆ 888-210-8216 (orders only) ◆ Fax: 425-644-9274

liteinfo@illumin.com ◆ www.illumin.com

Library of Congress Cataloging-in-Publication Data

Schmidt, Heidi Charissa, 1972 –
    Too many Murkles / written by Heidi Charissa Schmidt ; illustrated by Mary Gregg Byrne.
        p. cm.
    Summary: A young girl is able to solve a series of problems for her town by looking at
each from a different perspective.
    ISBN 0 – 9701907 – 7 – 8
    [1. Problem solving- -Fiction. 2. Perspective (Philosophy) - -Fiction.]   I. Byrne, Mary
Gregg, 1951 - ill. II. Title.
    PZ7.S35275To 2003
    [E] - -dc21

                                                        2002027519

Published in the United States of America

Printed in Singapore by Tien Wah Press

Book Designer: Molly Murrah, Murrah & Company, Kirkland, WA

Illumination Arts Publishing Company is a
member of Publishers in Partnership—replanting our nation's forests.

A portion of the profits from this book will be donated to The Children's Global Foundation, a non-profit organization dedicated to global peace and to helping homeless children worldwide.

This foundation was formed by Children's Global Village (CGV), an organization of leading architects, engineers, developers, builders, and media specialists working together to promote advancements in education and environmentally safe solutions to society's problems. CGV's goal is to develop spiritually-based cities of the future around the world. In addition to futuristic schools, homes, offices and business developments, each city will have a world-class theme park providing culturally diverse education and entertainment. For more information on CGV cities of the future, contact cgv@illumin.com.